It's hard to dedicate this book to one person, so I would like to thank my family: my beautiful wife and handsome son, my parents, my sisters and brother, my grandfather, my uncles and aunts, and my cousins. But especially my grandmother, Mattie Love Tuck. No one truly knows how close we were. I remember her singing spiritual hymns in the kitchen while making red velvet cake. She was and still is the Tuck family backbone.
—J. T.

For Esteban and Leticia, my children
—L. R.

SIMON & SCHUSTER BOOKS FOR YOUNG READERS • An imprint of Simon & Schuster Children's Publishing Division • 1230 Avenue of the Americas, New York, New York 10020 • Text copyright © 2011 by Justin Tuck • Illustrations copyright © 2011 by Leonardo Rodriguez • All rights reserved, including the right of reproduction in whole or in part in any form. • Simon & Schuster Books for Young Readers is a trademark of Simon & Schuster, Inc. • For information about special discounts for bulk purchases, please contact Simon & Schuster Special Sales at 1-866-506-1949 or business@simonandschuster.com. • The Simon & Schuster Speakers Bureau can bring authors to your live event. For more information or to book an event, contact the Simon & Schuster Speakers Bureau at 1-866-248-3049 or visit our website at www.simonspeakers.com. • Book design by Chloë Foglia • The text for this book is set in Family Dog. • The illustrations for this book are rendered in watercolor. Manufactured in China • 0611 SCP
2 4 6 8 10 9 7 5 3 1
Library of Congress Cataloging-in-Publication Data • Tuck, Justin. • Home-field advantage / Justin Tuck ; illustrated by Leonardo Rodriguez. — 1st ed. • p. cm. • Summary: New York Giants defensive end Justin Tuck observes that growing up with five sisters helped make him tough, and tells of when twins Christale and Tiffany gave him an unforgettable haircut. • ISBN 978-1-4424-0369-7 • 1. Tuck, Justin—Juvenile fiction. [1. Tuck, Justin—Fiction. 2. Haircutting—Fiction. 3. Brothers and sisters—Fiction. 4. Twins—Fiction. 5. Family life—Fiction. 6. Football—Fiction.] I. Rodriguez, Leonardo, 1969– ill. II. Title. PZ7.T8Hom 2011 • [E]—dc22 2010043733 • ISBN 978-1-4424-3429-5 (eBook)

JUSTIN TUCK'S
HOME-FIELD ADVANTAGE

Illustrated by

LEONARDO RODRIGUEZ

SIMON & SCHUSTER BOOKS FOR YOUNG READERS
NEW YORK LONDON TORONTO SYDNEY

My name is Justin Tuck, and I'm six feet five and weigh 274 pounds. I play defensive end for the New York Football Giants.

When people ask me how I got to be so tough, I say, "You'd be tough too, if you grew up with . . .

Wendy   Kimberly

...my five sisters!"

Christale   Tiffany   BRITTANY

They used to give me a hard time.

The twins, Christale and Tiffany, especially helped me to be extra tough.

Like the day they decided to give me a haircut.

"Your hair's getting kind of long," said Christale.

"We'll make you handsome so the girls will notice you," said Tiffany.

My older brother, Raleigh, laughed as he walked away. "You're on your own with this one, little man."

I wasn't sure at first that I needed a haircut.

"When was the last time you cut someone's hair?" I asked.

"We've watched Mama do it plenty of times," said Christale.

"There's nothing to it," said Tiffany.

They took a kitchen chair outside.

"Sit," said Christale. "We'll be done in a jiffy."

"Then won't you be the man," said Tiffany.

The twins seemed so sure they could do a good job that I sat.

Christale tied a towel around my neck and Tiffany went and got some scissors.

Then **snip, snip, snip.** First one twin, then the other started cutting.

"Can I see how I look?" I asked after a while.

"Not yet," said Christale.

"The sides aren't even," said Tiffany.

Snip, Snip, Snip. The twins kept cutting till I was worried that *all* my hair was lying on the grass.

"Whooeee," said Christale, reaching for the mirror.

Tiffany put her hand to her mouth to keep from giggling.

I stared at the mirror. I had never seen such a mangled bunch of hair in my whole life!

I ran inside and threw myself on my bed. I pulled my blanket over my head and stayed there for the rest of the day.

When Mama and Papa got home from work, they asked, "Where's Justin?"

Christale looked at Tiffany. Tiffany looked at Christale.

"In bed," they said.

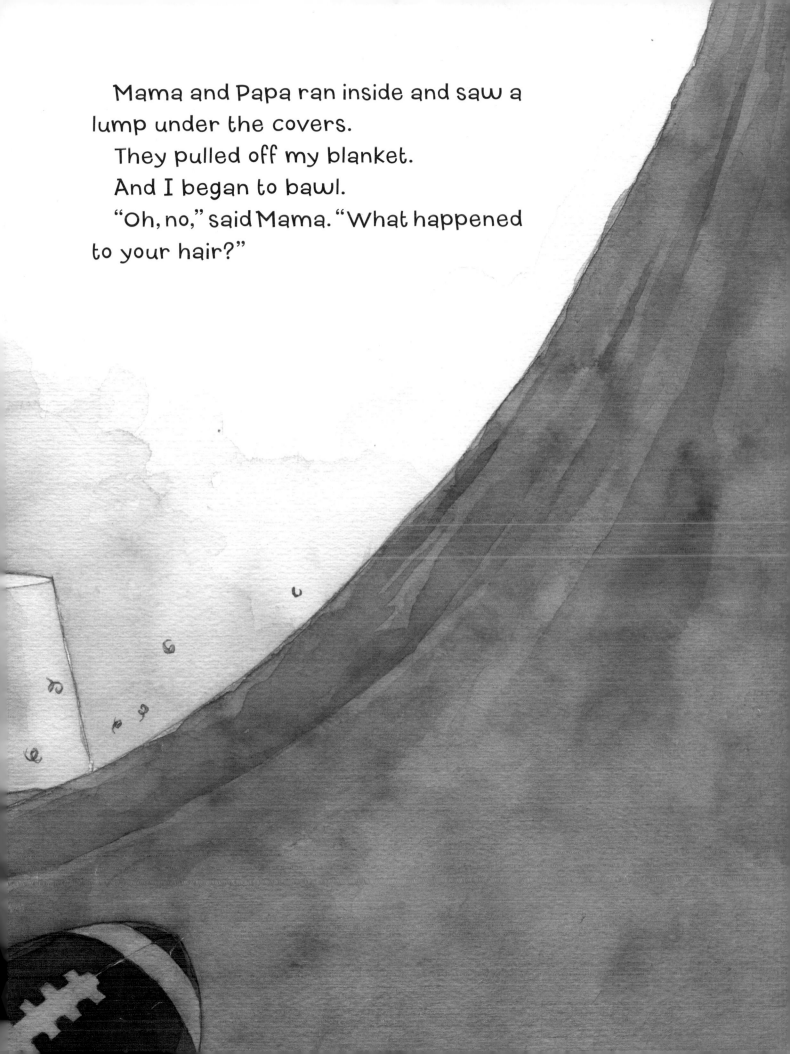

Mama and Papa ran inside and saw a
lump under the covers.
   They pulled off my blanket.
   And I began to bawl.
   "Oh, no," said Mama. "What happened
to your hair?"

"We didn't mean for it to turn out like a reverse mohawk," said Christale.
"Maybe we went a little too far," said Tiffany.

They turned to me.
"We're sorry, little bro—we were just messing around. You know we love you, right?"

And I did. Even when they did things like this, I knew they loved me and I loved them. We were a family and that's what family was all about.

It also helped that as I got older, it got harder and harder to push me around!

But maybe someday
I'll let them give me
another haircut . . .

. . . or maybe not!

ABOUT THE AUTHOR

At The University of Notre Dame (2001 to 2004), Justin was nicknamed The Freak by his teammates because of his athletic skill. He finished his Notre Dame career with 24.5 sacks and still holds several defensive records, including 43 tackles for loss and 13.5 sacks in a single season.

He played high school football at Central Coosa County High School in Alabama, where he was a quarterback before becoming a tight end and a defensive end. He earned Alabama Class 4A Player of the Year as a senior in 2000 and won two state championships for basketball. His twin sisters were also all-star basketball players.

In 2008 Justin and his wife, Lauran, founded Tuck's R.U.S.H. for Literacy to encourage children to Read, Understand, Succeed, and Hope. R.U.S.H. donates books and other reading materials to support children in the New York City and Central Alabama communities. Justin's parents believed in education, and by supporting literacy, the Tucks hope to encourage children to develop a love for books. As Justin says, "Academic success starts with reading and literacy."

Justin is now an All-Pro defensive end and defensive captain for the New York Football Giants in the National Football League. He was part of the 2008 Super Bowl–winning team.